Danny's Party

written and photographed
by
Mia Coulton

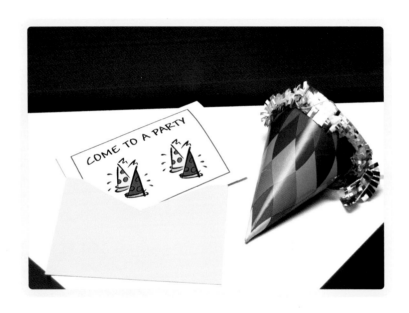

3

I am going

to a party.

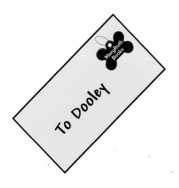

To Dooley

MaryRuth
Books

4

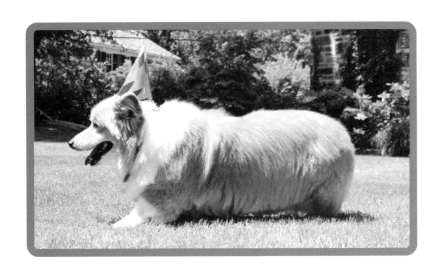

5

I am going

to a party.

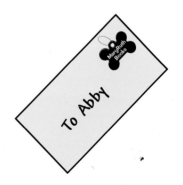

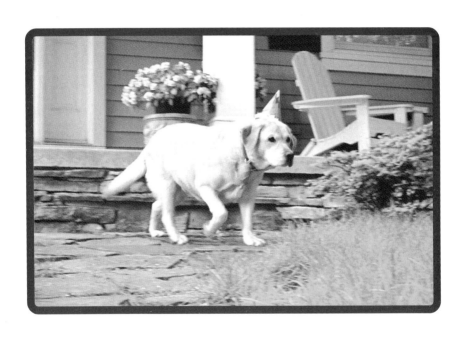

I am going

to a party.

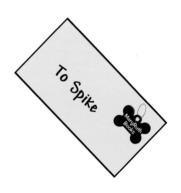

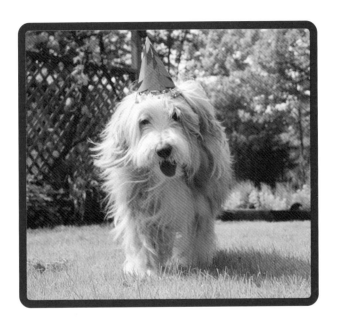

I am going

to a party.

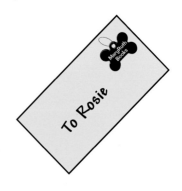

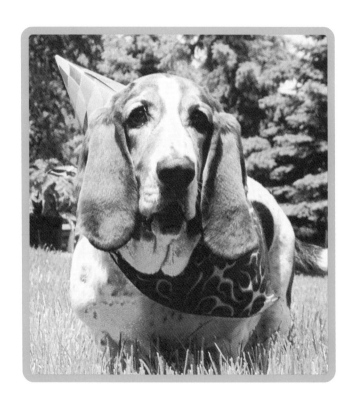

Happy birthday, Danny!

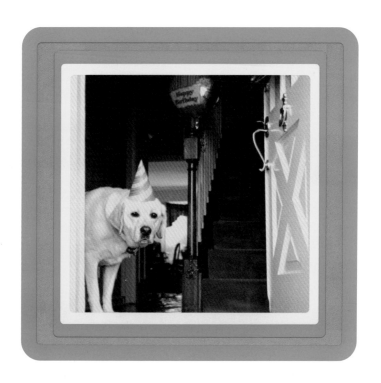